Sniffles and Surprises

Mermicorns®

Purrmaids

MeRMiCORns

4

Sniffles and Surprises

by Sudipta Bardhan-Quallen

illustrations by Vivien Wu

A STEPPING STONE BOOK™

Random House 🏠 New York

This is a work of fiction. Names, characters, places, and incidents either are the product of the author's imagination or are used fictitiously. Any resemblance to actual persons, living or dead, events, or locales is entirely coincidental.

Text copyright © 2022 by Sudipta Bardhan-Quallen
Cover art copyright © 2022 by Andrew Farley
Interior illustrations copyright © 2022 by Vivien Wu

Visit us on the Web!
rhcbooks.com

Educators and librarians, for a variety of teaching tools, visit us at
RHTeachersLibrarians.com

Library of Congress Cataloging-in-Publication Data
Names: Bardhan-Quallen, Sudipta, author. | Wu, Vivien, illustrator.
Title: Sniffles and surprises / by Sudipta Bardhan-Quallen ;
illustrations by Vivien Wu.
Description: First edition. | New York : Random House Children's Books, [2022] |
Series: Mermicorns ; 4 | "A Stepping Stone book" | Audience: Ages 6–9 |
Summary: "When Lily has to stay home sick from magic school she is worried her whole day is ruined, until her best friend Sirena and their kitten-mermaid pals visit with a surprise." —Provided by publisher
Identifiers: LCCN 2021006434 (print) | LCCN 2021006435 (ebook) |
ISBN 978-0-593-30882-0 (trade paperback) |
ISBN 978-0-593-30883-7 (library binding) | ISBN 978-0-593-30884-4 (ebook)
Subjects: CYAC: Mermaids—Fiction. | Unicorns—Fiction. | Sick—Fiction. |
Surprise—Fiction.
Classification: LCC PZ7.B25007 Sn 2022 (print) | LCC PZ7.B25007 (ebook) |
DDC [Fic]—dc23

Printed in the United States of America
10 9 8 7 6 5 4 3 2 1
First Edition

This book has been officially leveled by using
the F&P Text Level Gradient™ Leveling System.

Random House Children's Books supports the
First Amendment and celebrates the right to read.

To Victoria P.,
the dog-loving YouTube addict

1

*B*eep, *beep, beep, beep!*

Lily rubbed her eyes. She reached for the alarm clock. It was time to wake up to get ready for school.

But Lily was still very tired. Even though her sister Lotus was snoring, Lily felt like she couldn't stay awake! *I just need a little more sleep*, she thought. *I'll rest for two minutes.*

The next time Lily opened her eyes, it

was because Dad was calling her name. "Lily," Dad neighed. "Are you going to get dressed today?"

Lily threw off her blanket. "I was only sleeping for two more minutes," she said. But then she looked at the clock. "Oh no!" she cried. It wasn't two minutes later—it was twenty minutes later! "I'm going to be so late!"

"What happened?" Dad asked. "Did you forget to set your alarm?"

Lily shook her head. "I just feel a little tired," she said. She swam over to her father. But she was definitely moving more slowly than usual.

Dad checked Lily's forehead. "You have a bit of a fever," he said, frowning. "Let me get the thermometer."

"No," Lily cried. She shook her head. "I'm fine, real— *Achoo!*"

"That doesn't sound fine," Dad said.

Lily wanted to argue. But she sneezed again!

"Open up," Dad said, holding out the thermometer.

Lily let Dad put the thermometer in her mouth. After a few moments, there was a beep. "Now it's official," Dad said. "You have a fever. That means you need to get back to bed, young filly. No school for you."

"But, Dad!" Lily whined. "I can't miss school today. Ms. Trainor said we are going to learn exciting new magic!"

"You learn exciting new magic *every* day," Dad replied.

"It's not just the lesson!" Lily continued. "Sirena and I were planning to go to our clubhouse after school. We're supposed to meet some friends there."

Sirena was another mermicorn who lived in Seadragon Bay. They'd met right before they started at the Mermicorn Magic Academy. But they didn't really become friends until after their magic lessons began. Their teacher, Ms. Trainor, made them partners in class. They began spending time together to practice magic. Soon, they'd become best friends.

Sirena was the one who introduced Lily to the friends who were coming to the clubhouse. Their names were Shelly, Angel, and Coral. They were purrmaids from Kittentail Cove. Lily didn't get to see them every day. If she couldn't go to the clubhouse after school, she didn't know how long she'd have to wait until the next time they could all be together.

Dad patted Lily's shoulder. "Your temperature isn't very high," he said. "But you're definitely sick with something. And that means you could get other mermicorns sick if you are with them."

"I'll stay away from everyone!" Lily exclaimed. "Please, let me go to school." She didn't sneeze again. But she couldn't hold back some coughs!

Dad shook his head. "I'm afraid that just isn't safe to do. It's easy for a little cold to spread if mermicorns aren't careful. In a small classroom, it's really hard to stay far enough apart to keep everyone safe." He swam toward the bedroom door. "We'll tell Sirena you won't be swimming over this morning. And we'll call Ms. Trainor."

Lily frowned and turned her face away from Dad. She knew he was right. But that didn't make her like it. *This is so unfair,* she thought. *Being sick ruins everything!*

2

When Mom knocked on her door, Lily was still upset. She didn't want to look at anyone. She grabbed her blanket and pulled it over her head.

Mom swam to the bed. "I know you're not feeling well," she neighed. "I bet your head hurts from the fever."

Lily nodded.

"And your throat hurts from sneezing and coughing," Mom added.

Lily nodded again.

Mom gently pulled the blanket back. "And," she said, "I bet your heart hurts from disappointment."

Lily gulped. "I really wanted to see everyone at the clubhouse this afternoon," she mumbled.

"I know, Lily," Mom said. She patted Lily's hoof.

"I don't feel that bad," Lily muttered. "Dad is being way too careful."

"He's a doctor, Lily," Mom said. "If there's any mermicorn who knows what to do, it's him!"

"Can't Dad use magic to make me better?" Lily asked.

"Any parent in the world would make their children magically feel better if they could," Mom replied. "So if there is something we're *not* doing, it's because it isn't possible. There are just some things that magic can't do. Making a cold or a fever go away is one of them."

Lily frowned. "It's not fair! Are mermicorns trying to fix this?"

Mom nodded. "There are many mermicorn scientists who work very hard to find treatments for every kind of illness," she said.

"Is science the same as magic?" Lily asked.

Mom giggled. "Science can certainly feel magical! Sometimes, when someone doesn't understand all the science, it might make them think it's just all magic. But science is real, and it does wonderful things for the world."

"So if I can't go to school, what am I supposed to do all day?" Lily mumbled.

"You're supposed to rest," Mom said. "The more you take care of yourself now, the faster you'll get better." She smiled. "I do have some good news, though."

"What is—" Lily started.

Ding dong! Someone was at the door!

Mom smiled. "I wonder who that could be," she said. "Maybe Sirena?"

Lily frowned. "Why would Sirena be here?"

"Let's find out," Mom neighed. She floated to Lily's bedroom door.

Sirena swam up and said, "Good morning, Mrs. Farrier. Can I talk to Lily for a minute?"

"Of course you can talk to her," Mom said. "It's just important that you stay a safe distance away from her. We don't want you to catch any germs Lily might have."

Sirena waved from the doorway. "How are you feeling?" she asked.

"I think I'm all right," Lily said. "But my parents say I have to rest."

"They're probably right," Sirena said. "But don't worry. I'll take good notes for you during our lesson."

Lily frowned. "I'm not just missing class," she whined. "We were going to meet Shelly, Angel, and Coral at the club-house today! I'm not going to get to see them."

"We could video call you," Sirena said. "Or you could call us if you're feeling up to it."

"That's not the same," Lily mumbled.

"I know," Sirena said. "But it's better than nothing."

Mom came back and tapped Sirena's shoulder. "You probably need to get going," she said. "Your headmistress, Mrs. Falabella, gets crabby when her students aren't on time."

"I'll talk to you later, Lily!" Sirena called, waving goodbye.

Mom swam back to Lily's bed. "I spoke to Ms. Trainor," she said. She put her laptop on Lily's side table. "She said that you can still watch today's lesson."

"How?" Lily asked, frowning.

"You're not the only foal who seems

to have caught a cold," Mom said. She typed something on the keyboard. Then she clicked on a few things. Suddenly, a picture of Ms. Trainor floating in her classroom filled the screen. "Your teacher is going to record today's class. That way, you can watch it from home when you're feeling well enough. That could be today, or sometime over the weekend—or not at all if it doesn't work out. Ms. Trainor also said she'll go over everything with you when you are back in class. What do you think of that?"

Lily shrugged. "I guess it's fine."

Mom ruffled Lily's mane. "I think it's awfully nice of Ms. Trainor to arrange this for her sick students," she said.

"But that's not enough to turn a sick day into a good day," Lily said. "I don't know if there will be anything good about today."

Mom smiled. "Believe it or not, you can usually find something good in almost every day," she said. "So we'll just have to see how today works out."

Lily shrugged again.

"Now, take this medicine," Mom said. She plopped a pill into Lily's open mouth. The taste made Lily frown. "It tastes like blobfish that was left in the sun!" she cried.

"You've never tasted blobfish," Mom replied, laughing.

"It tastes really bad," Lily grumbled.

"Well, it will make you feel much better," Mom said. "You need to rest for a bit. Dad will wake you when the lesson starts."

"He won't forget, will he?" Lily asked. She settled into bed. She felt very tired again.

"Of course he won't!" Mom said. But Lily was already asleep!

3

Lily woke up to Dad stroking her mane. "How are you feeling, little girl?" he asked.

Lily stretched and yawned. She hated to admit it, but the nap and the medicine had really helped. "I feel much better now!" she said.

Dad laughed. "I guess that means I'm a pretty good doctor!" he said.

Lily stuck her tongue out at Dad and then grinned.

"I don't think you're well enough to get up and move around too much," Dad said. "Would you like to watch your lesson now? That's something you can do from bed." When she nodded, he opened the laptop on Lily's table.

"I need my notebook," Lily said.

"I'll get it," Dad said.

Soon, Lily was settled with everything she needed. They found the button for the video lesson and hit play. But the picture on the computer screen hadn't changed. "Do you think Ms. Trainor forgot to start the camera?" Lily asked.

Before Dad could answer, the screen changed. It started as a picture of Ms. Trainor's nose—very close up! "I hope she didn't teach from there," Lily said, giggling.

Luckily, Ms. Trainor backed away from the camera. She floated to her usual spot in the front of the classroom. Lily could see the backs of her classmates' heads. She could also see lots of empty chairs.

"Let's begin, class," Ms. Trainor neighed. "We have a lot of students absent today. They're not feeling well, so they are resting at home. But some of them wanted to listen in on our lesson. So I've got my video camera on." She pointed to the camera.

Sirena quickly turned around to wave at the camera. Lily knew she was waving to her.

"We've talked about how positive feelings can be magical," Ms. Trainor continued.

"Like happiness," Sirena said.

"Or bravery," Misty added.

Ms. Trainor smiled. "Today, we're going to learn about another positive feeling and how magical it can be." She wrote a word on the board: *determination*. "When you feel determined, you've decided that you are going to do something, no matter how hard it is," she said.

"When I was a student here at the Magic Academy, I was determined to be the president of my class."

"And were you?" Dory asked.

Ms. Trainor chuckled. "Actually, my best friend was elected class president."

Flipper raised his hoof. "If you didn't win, was your determination still positive?"

"Yes, it was," Ms. Trainor answered. "You can be determined without succeeding. Being determined means you believe in yourself. And that's very positive."

Lily nodded and scribbled notes onto her paper. Everything her teacher said made sense.

Sirena asked, "What if you're determined to do something that isn't good? Is that still a positive feeling?"

"I was waiting for that question," Ms.

SeaView

Trainor neighed. "That gets a little complicated. But feelings are complicated! A lot of the time, we don't know if the thing we want to do will turn out to be good or bad. Sometimes we want to do something good, and it turns out to be a mistake."

"Like when I tried to make breakfast

for my dad on his birthday!" Toby said. "I made such a mess, we had to go to a restaurant!"

Ms. Trainor laughed. "Sometimes, we can even try to do something that isn't so nice—but then it turns out to be the right thing! When I became a teacher, I didn't have the kindest reason. My sister was going to be a teacher, and I wanted to be better than her at something!"

"You're a great teacher, Ms. Trainor!" Misty exclaimed.

"Thank you!" Ms. Trainor replied. "I may have been inspired by a little jealousy and a little competitiveness. But then I discovered that I love teaching! And I've spent every day since then trying to be the best teacher I can be. The point is, we don't always know the result of our determination. But determination itself is usually a positive thing to feel."

In her room, Lily grinned. Ms. Trainor had a wonderful way of explaining things so that all her students could understand.

But then, Lily thought of something about the lesson that was bothering her. *What about when determination doesn't work?* This morning, she was determined to go to school. But she was stuck at home anyway.

Lily gulped. *What if my determination isn't magical enough?*

4

Lily was pretty worried about her question on determination. But she couldn't ask her teacher until she was better. She forced herself to go back to paying attention to Ms. Trainor.

"There are a lot of things you can do with determination—with or without magic," Ms. Trainor continued. "But since we are here at the Magic Academy, today's lesson will use magic!"

The students in class laughed.

"Today's lesson will show you how to move something through the water without touching it," Ms. Trainor said.

"Like Mrs. Booker does at the library?" Sirena asked. "She re-shelves books using magic."

"Exactly," Ms. Trainor said. "Let me demonstrate." She floated off to one side. There was something purple and orange on her desk. Lily knew exactly what it was: a royal starfish. They were rare, but the Farriers had one in their yard.

Ms. Trainor turned toward the desk. She closed her eyes and found her sparkle. She said, "Flippy fins and fishy face, move this to a brand-new place!" She pointed her horn toward the starfish and then toward the camera. The starfish floated up through the water and hovered right in front of the lens.

"Wow," Lily whispered. Ms. Trainor made it look so easy! She scribbled the magic words down in her notebook. When she looked back at the screen, Ms. Trainor was pointing her horn back at her desk. Once again, the starfish floated to where she was pointing. The students cheered when it landed.

SeaView

"Any questions?" Ms. Trainor asked.

"I have one," Toby said. "Would we ever have to carry anything again? Can't we use this magic for our backpacks?"

"Or our toys?" Aqua asked.

Ms. Trainor smiled. "It's tempting, isn't it?" she said. "We'd never have to lift a hoof if we could use magic all the time."

The mermicorns nodded. At home, Lily did, too.

"Unfortunately," Ms. Trainor continued, "we can't use magic all the time. Magic takes energy just like everything else. Imagine if you had to swim super fast all day long, every day."

"I'd be so tired," Sirena neighed. "And hungry!"

"Exactly," Ms. Trainor agreed. "You couldn't keep swimming super fast without eating and getting some sleep. If you used magic all day long, you'd be pretty worn out, too."

"I guess that means we should save this magic to move really heavy things," Flipper said.

"That brings up an interesting point," Ms. Trainor replied. "There are some things this magic can do, and other things that just can't be done. For example, it's much harder to move heavy things than it is to move things that weigh less."

That made perfect sense to Lily.

"Also," Ms. Trainor said, "you can only move something that you can see. Which means you can't magically move the homework you forgot at home and bring it to class." She winked. "Not that any of you would ever forget your homework!"

Everyone giggled.

Ms. Trainor looked directly into the camera. "I want all my sick students to get back to resting," she neighed. "We need you to get better quickly!"

Lily smiled. It felt like Ms. Trainor was talking directly to her. It almost felt like she was in the classroom!

"I think we should all practice together one time," Ms. Trainor continued. "Find a partner, everyone!"

Lily frowned. That feeling of being back in class disappeared pretty quickly. Even worse, practicing one time wouldn't be enough! In class, the students sometimes practiced all afternoon. *But there, I have a partner.* Usually that partner was Sirena. *Here, I'm all alone.*

Then Lily frowned even harder. She was by herself, but Sirena wasn't! On the screen, Lily saw that Sirena had floated

over to Aqua. She couldn't hear what they were saying. But it was clear that the two of them were going to practice together. Somehow, that made Lily feel even more lonely.

What if being sick means I'll lose more than one day at school? Lily thought. *What if it means I'll lose my best friend?*

5

There was a part of Lily that just wanted to go back to sleep. But she knew that she'd be disappointed later if she didn't watch the whole lesson. *I guess I'm determined to learn,* she thought.

On the screen, Ms. Trainor swam around the room. She was carrying a tray of mini cupcakes. She placed one in front of each student. "You can practice on these. See if you can magically move them toward your mouth!" After she'd given out all the mini cupcakes, she looked into the camera again. "If you're at home, and you feel well enough, you can pick something near you to try to move. But it's perfectly fine to just watch, too, if you don't feel up to it."

Lily looked around her room. There was a mane clip on her dresser. *It's not a cupcake,* she thought. *But I guess it'll do.*

"Is everyone ready?" Ms. Trainor asked.

Lily watched her classmates. One by one, they each found their sparkle easily. When Lily tried, though, it didn't work. She couldn't find her sparkle at all! *I can't do this right now.* It was hard to feel positive feelings when she felt so far away from her friends.

Lily decided she'd just watch the

mermicorns in class. They started saying the magic words. Soon, mini cupcakes were floating all around. But it was clear that they needed more practice! Cinnamon's cupcake missed her mouth and ended up in her mane. Marlin's cupcake floated up slowly, but then it fell—upside down! It was smashed on his desk.

SeaView

Sirena and Aqua were doing fine, though. Lily saw that they'd figured out the magic easily. *Maybe if I was there in class, I would be able to do the magic, too*, she thought.

"That was a great try!" Ms. Trainor exclaimed. "Although, most of you are going to have to practice some more." She winked. "But that's all right. Practice makes perfect!" She looked into the camera again. "For my students who have been watching from home, please remember that I don't expect you to understand this lesson all by yourselves. When you get back to the Magic Academy, I'll go over it again and answer any questions you have. I'm glad I could share this lesson with you while you're at home. But make sure you work on getting well again.

That's more important than working on any new magic."

Lily bit her lip. She was glad Ms. Trainor said all that. It made her feel better about having trouble with the lesson.

The class waved goodbye. "Hope you all feel better soon!" Ms. Trainor said. Just before the camera turned off, Lily saw Sirena holding up a sign. It read, I MISS YOU, LILY! That made her smile. *Miss you, too, Sirena,* she thought.

As Lily closed her laptop, Mom opened the bedroom door. "Is the lesson over?"

Lily nodded. "It just finished."

"Good," Mom said, "because you need to take more medicine!"

"Not the blobfish medicine!" Lily groaned.

"Oh, stop being such a drama queen-fish," Mom said.

Lily rolled her eyes. But she let Mom put the pill in her mouth. It still tasted terrible!

"How did the lesson go?" Mom asked.

"I don't know," Lily replied. "I had a hard time even finding my sparkle."

Mom said, "It's not easy to find positive feelings when you're sick."

"It's not just that." Lily sighed. "It's lonely being here when all my friends are in class."

Mom patted Lily's shoulder. "I know," she said.

"And it's a little boring," Lily added. "Everyone else will be practicing magic. I don't have anything to do."

"I have an idea," Mom said. "Why don't we watch some shell-ivision together? I'll make us a snack, too. I think *Seal of Fortune* is on."

"*Seal of Fortune!*" Lily cried. "We haven't watched that together in ages."

"It's hard to watch shell-ivision together when you're at school and I'm at work," Mom neighed. "So this is a treat for you *and* me."

6

Lily settled on the sofa with a plate of mango and pineapple slices. During *Seal of Fortune*, Lily guessed the answer to every puzzle! Then they watched *Shark Tank* and *Bubble Dare*.

"What now?" Mom asked.

Lily held up the empty plate. "More snacks?"

"I'm glad your appetite is back," Mom said. "I'll get us some more from the kitchen. You figure out what we can watch next."

When Mom left, Lily realized that *Eel or No Eel* was on soon. *But it's on a different channel,* she thought. The remote control was on the table by Mom's chair. It was too far away to reach from her seat.

Lily really didn't want to get up. *I could wait for Mom.* But she heard Mom's shell phone ring, which meant she wasn't coming back right away. And *Eel or No Eel* was about to start.

Then Lily had an idea. She closed her eyes and tried to find her sparkle. This time, it worked! Then she opened her eyes and said, "Flippy fins and fishy face, move this to a brand-new place!" She pointed her horn at the remote control and then at the sofa.

At first, nothing happened. But Lily felt

so determined! She kept concentrating on the remote control. Suddenly, the remote floated up off the table. *It's working!* Lily thought. She grinned as the remote drifted toward her. When it was close enough, she reached out and grabbed it. "I did it!" she shouted.

"Did what?" Mom asked, swimming back into the room. She saw Lily holding the remote control. "Did

you get up to get that? You could have waited for me."

Lily's grin got even bigger. "I didn't need to get up," she replied. "I used magic!"

"That's amazing!" Mom exclaimed. "Was this what today's lesson was about?"

Lily nodded.

Mom smiled. "I'm so proud of you."

"Watch this," Lily said. She quickly switched to the channel for *Eel or No Eel*. Then she found her sparkle and said the magic words again. This time, she made the remote control float out of her hands. She pointed her horn at the side table.

The remote moved through the water and landed on . . . the floor! Lily shrugged. "I guess I still need a little practice!"

The mermicorns laughed. "I think it's great you learned new magic from home," Mom said.

"I agree," Lily said. "But we can talk about the lesson later." She pointed to the shell-ivision. "Now it's time for *Eel or No Eel*!"

As the show was ending, Lily felt her eyes closing. Without even realizing, she fell asleep on the sofa. She didn't wake up until her big sister Lotus came home from the Magic Academy.

"Are you feeling better, Lily?" Lotus asked from across the room. "How was your day?"

"I am," Lily answered, "and it wasn't too bad. I watched the lesson from class today on the computer, and I got to watch shell-ivision with— *Achoo!*"

"You're still sneezing," Lotus said. "So stay away from me! I can't get sick."

Mom swam to Lotus with the thermometer. "No one *wants* to get sick," she said. "Let's make sure you haven't caught the same cold."

Lotus rolled her eyes. But she let Mom put the thermometer in her mouth. When Mom took it out, she said, "No fever."

"Good," Lotus neighed, "because I have plans with my friends this afternoon."

Lily frowned. *I had plans with my friends, too. That's all ruined now.* She was glad that her sister wasn't sick. But she hated how lonely it was to be the only one who was.

"I'm going to go back to bed, Mom," Lily mumbled.

"All right, Lily," Mom replied. She smiled. "You'll be better soon, I promise."

Lily nodded without looking at her mother. She knew Mom was trying to

help. But thinking about later didn't change how things felt now.

Lily settled into her bed again. She noticed the shell phone on her side table. She sighed. *Sirena said that she would call,* she thought. She checked the clock. Sirena should be at the clubhouse already. The purrmaids might be there, too. *Maybe I'll call Sirena instead.*

Lily dialed Sirena's number. The phone rang once . . . twice . . . three times. But Sirena didn't pick up! *She must be having too much fun with Shelly, Coral, and Angel.* She frowned. *And I'm missing it!*

7

Lily's mood was as dark as a thunder-cloud. It was bad enough to be sick and to miss being with her classmates. But missing out on a visit from the purrmaids was the worst! *I wish I could use moving magic to move my friends from the club-house to here,* she thought.

Lily squeezed her eyes shut to keep from crying. That's why she didn't see anything near her bedroom window. She almost jumped out of bed when she heard someone knocking on the glass! She swam over to see who it was. Then she gasped. There was a mermicorn floating in her yard!

"Sirena?" Lily asked, frowning. Sirena floated back from the window so Lily could open it. That would make it easier to talk. "What are you doing here? And why are you all alone?"

"She's not!" someone said.

But Lily didn't see anyone else. "Who was that?"

Sirena giggled. "I'm sorry, I forgot something. I need you to do me a favor."

"What?" Lily asked. "I'm so confused."

Sirena pointed to where the voice had come from. "Can you make someone un-invisible?"

"Who?" Lily asked.

"Just do it," Sirena said. "You'll see in a minute. And it might just be a few someones."

Lily's eyes grew wide. She had a guess about who Sirena had brought—but she was afraid to hope too much!

"Well?" Sirena said. "Are you going to help?"

Lily nodded. She closed her eyes and found her sparkle right away. Then she said, "Lobster claw, penguin tears, make the missing reappear!"

Lily watched sparkles swirl around and around. It started as one big cloud. But then, the sparkles started to swirl around three smaller areas in the water. When the sparkles disappeared, Lily saw three kitten mermaids. She gasped. "Shelly! Coral! Angel!" she exclaimed. "You're here!"

"We couldn't come to Seadragon Bay and *not* see you!" Angel said.

"I was so upset I couldn't go to the clubhouse," Lily said. "I can't believe you came to me!"

"Sirena told us you were sick," Coral said. "Are you feeling any better?"

Lily smiled. "I *am*," she replied. "I was really tired earlier. But my energy is back now."

"So, can you come play with us?" Shelly asked.

Lily's smile faded away. "We can't play together," she mumbled. "I'm still sneezing sometimes, so I'm stuck in here. I can't even go outside because I might get you sick!"

Sirena scratched her mane. "There have to be things we can do together—without actually *being* together."

The girls thought silently for a moment. Then Coral exclaimed. "I know! We could play Sea Horse Says."

"What's that?" Lily asked.

"It's a really fun game!" Shelly said. "We pick someone to be the sea horse. She will tell us to do something, like float upside down or spin around two times. Then we have to do it."

"But only if she says, 'Sea horse says'! Those are the magic words," Angel purred. "If she says them and we don't follow her instructions, we're out."

"But if she doesn't say the magic words and we do the thing anyway, then we're out, too!" Coral added.

"The last one floating is the winner," Shelly said.

Angel turned toward Lily. "You could be the sea horse, Lily. You can give the

instructions while we listen from here."

"That really is a *paw-some* idea!" Lily exclaimed. "Let's start!"

The first game of Sea Horse Says ended very quickly. Lily said, "Touch your tail." Sirena, Angel, and Shelly all followed the instructions. Coral was the only one who noticed that Lily hadn't said the magic words.

"Coral wins!" Lily exclaimed.

"Awwwww," Angel groaned.

"You should've been paying more attention," Coral said, giggling.

"Can we play again?" Shelly asked. "It didn't even get fun yet!"

"Of course," Lily said. "Everyone get ready."

They played Sea Horse Says five more times. That way everyone got to win once—and Coral got to win again! Then Lily said, "Let's play something new." She leaned over and grabbed her shell phone. "Can we play Freeze Dance?"

"Yes!" all her friends exclaimed.

"I'll play the music from here," Lily said. "When it stops, you all have to freeze. If you don't, then you're out."

Lily played the first song. It was Neighlor Swift's "Wildest Streams." Lily's friends danced through the whole song.

Then she played "You Belong at Sea"—the whole thing, again. By the time Lily started "Sharks Fly," Coral said, "Umm, Lily, are we playing Freeze Dance or just dancing?"

"Sorry!" Lily said, laughing. "I like her songs too much! I didn't want to stop them!"

"Maybe we should take a break and just listen to some music?" Shelly asked.

Angel nodded. "I agree! I'm getting a little tired from all this dancing!"

"That's a good idea," Sirena said. "We can think of what to play next, too."

Lily grinned. "I'll start the song again!"

8

Lily's friends sat down in her yard and listened to two more Neighlor Swift songs. Then Shelly played a song by Kelpy Sharkson called "Shark Side." "Turns out we were more than a little tired!" Angel joked.

Everyone giggled.

Lily said, "I'm a little hungry, too. I wish I had a snack. How about you guys?"

Before anyone could answer, someone

knocked on Lily's door. "It's me," Mom said. She floated into the room with a plate of kelp cookies. "I brought you something to eat. And I sent Lotus outside to bring some to your friends."

Lily's eyes grew wide. "That's the second wish I've made today that has come true!" she exclaimed.

"I told you that you'd be able to find something good about today!" Mom exclaimed, smiling. "Now, I have a question for you. I recognized Sirena outside. But your other friends—are they *purrmaids*?"

Lily nodded. "They are!" she answered. Then she frowned. Before Lily had met Angel, Coral, and Shelly, she hadn't been completely sure purrmaids were even real. "But, Mom, how do you know about purrmaids?"

Mom laughed. "You're not the only one who can make friends all around the ocean!" she said. "When I was your age, I had a purrmaid pen pal. Her name was Azurine Harbor, and she was from Kittentail Cove."

"*My* friends are from Kittentail Cove!" Lily neighed. "Why didn't you ever say you had purrmaid friends?"

"I guess it never came up," Mom replied. "You aren't usually curious about my friends."

"That's because you do boring mom things," Lily said.

Mom laughed again. "Well, I'm going to want to hear all about your friends when you feel better and we can really talk," she said. "Maybe you can find out if they know Azurine!"

Lily headed back toward the window. She wanted to tell everyone that Lotus would be out with a snack. Suddenly, she realized something. *Lotus is expecting me to have friends over. But she's not expecting* purrmaids! The first time Lily met kitten mermaids, she was a little afraid of them. What if Lotus saw them and got really scared?

Lily couldn't go out to take the cookies

from her sister. That could get everyone sick. There was no time to explain everything to Lotus, either. She thought about having the purrmaids hide or using invisibility magic on them. *But I don't want them to think I'm embarrassed of them!* She leaned out her window to see what Lotus would do.

Sirena and the purrmaids were still sitting in the sand. Lotus was swimming toward them. But Lily's friends didn't see her.

Luckily, Lotus didn't see *them*, either. That's because she was only looking at her shell phone screen. *As usual!* Lily thought. Then she smiled. Maybe her sister wasn't going to find out that purrmaids were real. *Not today, at least!*

Lotus placed a tray of kelp cookies on the sand between Coral and Angel.

"These are for you," she said. But she still didn't look up from her shell phone screen!

"Thank you," Sirena answered. But Lotus was already swimming away.

"Sorry about my sister," Lily said. "She's always on her shell phone."

Shelly grinned. "My sisters are like that, too!"

"I hope when we get older, we won't just be on our phones all day," Sirena said.

"That would be *so* boring, wouldn't it?" Lily agreed.

"I'm glad your sister was only looking at her shell phone," Angel purred.

Lily frowned. "Why?"

"Because these cookies are too good!" Angel exclaimed, giggling. "I'm glad she didn't eat any!"

Lily couldn't believe how much fun she was having. Even though her friends were outside and she was inside, they were laughing and joking and playing games. It was a different way to hang out—but somehow, it still worked. The best part was, her friends couldn't catch whatever germs she had. That meant no one would get sick because of her.

Mom was right, she thought. You could find something good in every day. Even a sick day! All you needed were wonderful friends!

9

It didn't take long for all the cookies to disappear. In fact, the entire afternoon seemed to fly by. When Lily looked at the clock, it was late. "It's almost five," she said. "You guys probably have to go home soon."

The purrmaids nodded. "We have to be home by dinner," Coral said. "And it's a long swim back to Kittentail Cove."

"I understand," Lily said quietly.

"We probably have time for one more game," Shelly said.

"What do you want to play, Lily?" Angel asked.

Lily thought for a moment. Then she spied a flash of purple and orange. It was the royal starfish! It was tucked under the back fence.

Suddenly, Lily had a great idea. "Let's play Wetter or Drier," she said. "I'll pick the target." She already knew the royal starfish would be perfect for her friends to look for! "Whoever finds it wins!"

"Let's get started," Shelly said.

"Just make sure you pick something really cool for us to find," Angel purred.

Lily grinned. "I see something with orange edges," she neighed.

The other girls looked all around.

There were a few clownfish swimming near the window of Lily's parents' bedroom. Coral and Angel headed there.

"Drier," Lily said.

Shelly found a conch shell in the sand in the middle of the yard.

"Drier," Lily said.

Sirena floated over to the back fence—but she turned the wrong way! She stopped next to an orange-peel sea slug.

Lily frowned. "You're all drier," she said.

"The same amount drier?" Angel asked. "Who is the closest?"

"Sirena is," Lily replied.

Everyone swam over to Sirena. They looked around again. Then Shelly exclaimed, "I think I see it!" She swam to . . . an orange mushroom coral! "Is this what we're looking for?"

Lily shook her head. "Even drier than before."

Shelly bent over to pick up an orange scallop shell. "Is this it?"

"Very dry," Lily said.

"Is it Coral?" Angel asked. "She's orange. Are we looking for Coral?"

Coral elbowed Angel while Lily giggled and said, "No, you're not looking for Coral."

"Give us another clue," Sirena said.

"I see something with orange edges," Lily said, "and a purple middle."

Sirena grinned. "I know what we're looking for!" she exclaimed. She swam along the back fence. But she swam right past the royal starfish. When she finally stopped, she said, "Is this it?" She pointed to a flame angelfish. It had an orange body with black stripes. It also had purple fins.

Lily rolled her eyes. "That isn't purple in the middle and orange on the edges!"

Sirena shrugged. "Yeah, I guess the colors are flipped."

"By the way," Lily neighed, "you were wetter for a minute. But you ended up as dry as seaweed left in the sun!"

The girls began to search again. Angel showed Lily a little red crab. "Are we looking for this?" she asked.

"That's not orange or purple," Lily said, shaking her head.

"Good," Angel purred. "No one wants to mess with a crab!"

Lily's friends seemed to pick up everything in the yard—except for the royal starfish! "Dry, dry, dry!" Lily shouted.

"Maybe it's time to give up," Coral said. "I'm getting a little tired."

"Me too," Shelly added.

Lily frowned. Her friends weren't having any fun. It had been a really great afternoon so far. She wanted it to end with something fun, too.

Suddenly, Lily had an idea. *The magic we learned today!* she thought. She could move the royal starfish to somewhere her friends were sure to find it. She leaned out the window and looked everywhere.

She spotted the empty cookie tray on the sand. *Perfect!*

Lily shouted, "Can you try one more time? I'll give you another clue."

The girls nodded.

"Please swim slowly toward the cookie tray," Lily continued.

"The cookie tray?" Sirena asked. "But that's where we started."

"Just trust me," Lily said. "And move very, very slowly."

Everyone swam slowly toward the tray.

Lily smiled and found her sparkle. She said, "Flippy fins and fishy face, move this to a brand-new place!" She pointed her horn at the royal starfish and then at the empty tray. The starfish floated up.

By then, the other girls had reached the tray. Shelly bent down and grabbed it. "There's nothing orange here," she said.

Lily kept concentrating. The starfish floated closer and closer.

But then, something unexpected happened. All of Lily's friends' heads were blocking the tray! Instead of landing on the empty cookie tray, the starfish ended up . . . in Sirena's mane!

"Ouch!" Sirena yelped. "What was that?"

Coral picked the royal starfish out of Sirena's mane. "Is this what we were looking for?"

Lily laughed. "Yes!"

"How did this starfish get into Sirena's mane?" Angel asked. "I've never seen starfish move like that."

Sirena grinned at Lily. "I think Lily used magic," she said. "It's new magic

we just learned today. Even though Lily wasn't in class, she has figured out how to do it."

"That's because I watched the lesson on my computer," Lily said.

"It's so cool that mermicorns can do magic," Shelly said.

"Maybe next time you could try to teach us some magic," Angel purred.

"I don't know," Coral said. Her eyes were wide. "That might be against the rules."

Everyone except Coral giggled.

Angel asked, "So, does that mean Lily won the game?"

Lily shook her head. "I think we just need to play again—when you guys come to Seadragon Bay again."

"That's a fin-tastic idea," Sirena said.

"For now," Lily said, "someone needs

to put the starfish back in his spot over by the fence. And then you guys should get home. If you're late, you might get into trouble—and then there might never be a next time!"

10

Lily was so happy that she'd gotten to see Sirena and the purrmaids. She didn't even complain when Dad brought her blobfish medicine before bed!

"I heard you had an exciting afternoon," Dad said. "You got to play with your friends?"

Lily nodded. "They came over," she said. "They stayed in the yard, and I talked to them through the window. It wasn't the same as what we normally do. But it was still fun." She scratched her mane. "I wasn't expecting that."

"I guess you learned something from being sick," Dad said.

"I learned moving magic, too," Lily said. "I watched Ms. Trainor's lesson."

"That's wonderful," Dad said.

"I do have a question, though," Lily said. "Can I go to school tomorrow?"

Dad ruffled her mane. "I don't think so," he neighed.

Lily frowned. "Why not?"

"Well," Dad replied, "you need to be feeling better for a bit longer before you can go back to class. That's to make sure you don't get anyone else sick." He grinned. "Also, tomorrow is Saturday, so no one would be at the Magic Academy anyway!"

Lily rolled her eyes. "Dad!" she groaned.

"Get ready for bed," Dad said. "The more you rest, the less time you'll spend sick." He kissed her forehead and swam out of her room.

Lily was fluffing her pillow when her shell phone rang. It was a video call from Sirena!

"Hello," Lily said, answering the phone.

"Hi, Lily," Sirena said. Her camera was on. But Lily couldn't see her face. And it looked like Sirena was carrying the phone somewhere.

"The camera isn't pointing the right way, Sirena," Lily said.

"I know!" Sirena exclaimed. "I have to show you something."

Lily watched as Sirena took the phone out to her family's oyster garden. She spun around slowly so Lily could see everything. "I realized that we're supposed to be picking out new pearls today. You get one for being good at moving magic. And I get two—one for the moving magic and one because I finally figured out how to turn purrmaids invisible!"

"But I can't go to your house," Lily said, frowning. "You know I'm sick."

"Of course I know that," Sirena said, looking into the camera. "That's why I'm showing you the whole garden. You decide which oyster you want. I'll open it for you so you can see. And then I'll give it to you when you're better!"

"That's a different way to keep our tradition going," Lily said.

"That's true," Sirena replied. "But we get to *keep* the tradition going. That's the most important part!"

Lily looked out at the garden. Then she remembered what Ms. Trainor said. *You can only move something you can see.* Even though she wasn't there with Sirena, she *could* see the oysters on the screen. *Maybe I could try something.*

Lily concentrated on an oyster that

was right next to Sirena's tail. She picked one that was small so it wouldn't be too hard to move. She thought about everything that happened that day. How her friends surprised her so she wouldn't be lonely. How they figured out a way to play together while keeping everyone safe from getting sick. How she was able to use magic to move the royal starfish when her friends couldn't find it.

Her horn began to sparkle without Lily even having to try too hard. Then she closed her eyes and whispered, "Flippy fins and fishy face, move this to a brand-new place!"

"Are you going to tell me which oyster to pick out for you?" Sirena asked.

"Just wait a minute," Lily neighed. She opened her eyes. She watched the screen carefully.

At first, nothing happened. Even Sirena stayed still. But then Lily saw something moving over Sirena's shoulder. She narrowed her eyes and concentrated.

A moment later, Lily's oyster was floating right in front of Sirena's face.

Sirena's eyes grew wide. She reached for the floating oyster. "How did you do that?"

"Magic!" Lily replied, laughing.

Sirena laughed, too. Then she propped the camera up so she could open the oyster shell. "Look at this!" she exclaimed. It was a shimmering silver pearl!

"That's amazing!" Lily said. "Now show me yours!"

Sirena closed her eyes. She said the magic words. Just like before, an oyster floated up toward her. She grabbed it, and then she said the magic words again. She moved a second oyster through the water.

"Good job, Sirena!" Lily said.

Sirena smiled. She opened the oysters and showed Lily. "Two pink pearls," she said.

"I love them," Lily said.

"Call me when you're feeling better," Sirena said. "I'll bring you your pearl."

The girls said good night. Lily settled

into her bed. She closed her eyes, thinking about the new silver pearl. She couldn't wait to add it to her necklace. Every time she looked at it, she'd remember this sick day. *The way my friends and I were able to have fun even though we couldn't be together,* she thought, *has been the most magical thing of all!*

Meet more friends from around the ocean!

Read on for a sneak peek!

"Let's get our guests home," Dad said. "They need to get settled. Tomorrow is a big day!"

The purrmaids and grrrmaids swam to Shelly's house. Mrs. Lake had a fin-tastic dinner waiting for them. "I've set out plates for everyone," she said. "Come sit down. I'm sure the Atwaters are hungry after their trip."

"Where should I sit, Shelly?" Leeza asked.

Shelly pulled out a chair. "How about here?" she suggested.

"Grrr-eat!" Leeza replied.

Before Shelly could sit down next to Leeza, Angel plopped into Shelly's chair. Angel didn't even seem to notice that Shelly was trying to sit there! Shelly scowled.

Coral was already sitting on Leeza's other side. So Shelly had to sit next to Angel. *That's all right,* she thought. *Angel and Coral will be going home soon. Then I can talk to Leeza all I want!*

The purrmaids started to eat all the yummy food. But the kittens still found time to ask Leeza questions.

"Do you have any brothers or sisters?" Coral asked.

Leeza nodded. "I have three older sisters," she said.

"That's a lot like me," Shelly said. She pointed to her older sisters, Tempest and Gale. "It's not easy being the youngest."

"I a-grrr-ee!" Leeza said.

"Who's your favorite singer?" Angel asked.

"I don't know if I have a favorite one.

I really like the Spice Grrr-ls," Leeza said. "And I also listen to Kelpy Sharkson."

Shelly's eyes grew wide. "I *love* Kelpy Sharkson! I even got to sing with her once!"

When it was time for dessert, Mom tapped Shelly on the shoulder. "We need your help."

Shelly nodded. They were having beach banana jelly served on mango slices. It was a recipe Shelly had invented when her class visited Coastline Farm. Beach bananas grew on land, so not many purrmaids used them in their cooking. Shelly thought that grrrmaids might not use them often, either!

Shelly arranged the mango slices on each plate. She put a small scoop of jelly on each one. Then she cut a piece of mango into the shape of a heart. That was the purr-fect finishing touch.

When everyone had a plate, Dad announced, "Dessert is served!"

Chef Atwater took one bite and grinned. "This is fin-credible!" he exclaimed. "I've never tasted anything like this!"

Dad winked at Shelly. "My daughter and her friends actually came up with this recipe," he purred.

"I could eat this fur-ever," Leeza said.

Shelly smiled. "Thank you!"